P9-CFL-328

A Note to Parents and Caregivers:

Read-it! Readers are for children who are just starting on the amazing road to reading. These beautiful books support both the acquisition of reading skills and the love of books.

The RED LEVEL presents familiar topics using common words and repeating sentence patterns.
The BLUE LEVEL presents new ideas using a larger vocabulary and varied sentence structure.
The YELLOW LEVEL presents more challenging ideas, a broad vocabulary, and wide variety in sentence structure.

When sharing a book with your child, read in short stretches, pausing often to talk about the pictures. Have your child turn the pages and point to the pictures and familiar words. And be sure to reread favorite stories or parts of stories.

There is no right or wrong way to share books with children. Find time to read with your child and pass on the legacy of literacy.

Adria F. Klein, Ph.D.
Professor Emeritus
California State University
San Bernardino, California

First American edition published in 2003 by
Picture Window Books
5115 Excelsior Boulevard
Suite 232
Minneapolis, MN 55416
1-877-845-8392
www.picturewindowbooks.com

First published in Great Britain by Franklin Watts, 96 Leonard Street, London, EC2A 4XD
Text © Anne Cassidy 2000
Illustration © Philip Norman 2000

Printed in the United States of America.
1 2 3 4 5 6 08 07 06 05 04 03

Library of Congress Cataloging-in-Publication Data
Cassidy, Anne.
  Cleo and Leo / written by Anne Cassidy ; illustrated by Philip Norman.
    p. cm. — (Read-it! readers)
  Summary: Ben and Mom lose Grandma's dog Cleo but come up with a possible solution.
  ISBN 1-4048-0049-2
  [1. Dogs—Fiction. 2. Lost and found possessions—Fiction. 3. Grandmothers—Fiction.] I.
Norman, Philip, ill. II. Title. III. Series.
  PZ7.C26857 Cl 2003
  [E]—dc21   2002072291

PiCTURE WiNDOW BOOKS

Cleo and Leo

Written by Anne Cassidy

Illustrated by Philip Norman

Reading Advisors:
Adria F. Klein, Ph.D.
Professor Emeritus, California State University
San Bernardino, California

Ruth Thomas
Durham Public Schools
Durham, North Carolina

R. Ernice Bookout
Durham Public Schools
Durham, North Carolina

Picture Window Books
Minneapolis, Minnesota

When Grandma went out
for the day, Cleo stayed
with Mom and Ben.

"Look after Cleo,"
Grandma said.

"She is very special."

Cleo was sad. She looked for Grandma in the yard,

in the kitchen,

and out of the window.

Ben felt sorry for Cleo.

He took her outside to play soccer.

"Oh no!" shouted Ben.

"Cleo is running away!"

Mom and Ben looked for Cleo in the street.

Then they knocked on all the doors.

"Grandma will be very upset," said Mom.

"Cleo is very special."

"Let's go to the animal shelter," said Ben.

"Maybe someone found Cleo."

At the animal shelter, Ruby
showed them around.

Ben couldn't see Cleo
anywhere.

"We found this little dog last week," said Ruby.

"His name is Leo."

"I've got an idea!" said
Ben.

Mom, Ben, and Ruby had
to get Leo ready.

Mom and Ben took Leo
to Grandma's house.

Grandma looked surprised.

"But Cleo is here!"
said Grandma.

"She was waiting for me
when I got home."

Now Grandma has two
dogs, Cleo and Leo.

They are both very special.

Red Level

The Best Snowman, by Margaret Nash 1-4048-0048-4
Bill's Baggy Pants, by Susan Gates 1-4048-0050-6
Cleo and Leo, by Anne Cassidy 1-4048-0049-2
Felix on the Move, by Maeve Friel 1-4048-0055-7
Jasper and Jess, by Anne Cassidy 1-4048-0061-1
The Lazy Scarecrow, by Jillian Powell 1-4048-0062-X
Little Joe's Big Race, by Andy Blackford 1-4048-0063-8
The Little Star, by Deborah Nash 1-4048-0065-4
The Naughty Puppy, by Jillian Powell 1-4048-0067-0
Selfish Sophie, by Damian Kelleher 1-4048-0069-7

Blue Level

The Bossy Rooster, by Margaret Nash 1-4048-0051-4
Jack's Party, by Ann Bryant 1-4048-0060-3
Little Red Riding Hood, by Maggie Moore 1-4048-0064-6
Recycled!, by Jillian Powell 1-4048-0068-9
The Sassy Monkey, by Anne Cassidy 1-4048-0058-1
The Three Little Pigs, by Maggie Moore 1-4048-0071-9

Yellow Level

Cinderella, by Barrie Wade 1-4048-0052-2
The Crying Princess, by Anne Cassidy 1-4048-0053-0
Eight Enormous Elephants, by Penny Dolan 1-4048-0054-9
Freddie's Fears, by Hilary Robinson 1-4048-0056-5
Goldilocks and the Three Bears, by Barrie Wade 1-4048-0057-3
Mary and the Fairy, by Penny Dolan 1-4048-0066-2
Jack and the Beanstalk, by Maggie Moore 1-4048-0059-X
The Three Billy Goats Gruff, by Barrie Wade 1-4048-0070-0